P9-CLR-332

WITHDRAWN

3/26/5

MORRIS AREA PUBLIC LIBRARY
604 Liberty St.
Morris, IL 60450
(815) 942-6880

THE CROSSOVER

BY KWAME ALEXANDER

Houghton Mifflin Harcourt
Boston   New York

MORRIS AREA LIBRARY

*For Big Al and Barbara,
also known as Mom and Dad*

Copyright © 2014 by Kwame Alexander

All rights reserved. For information about permission to reproduce selections from this book, write to Permissions, Houghton Mifflin Harcourt Publishing Company, 215 Park Avenue South, New York, New York 10003.

www.hmhco.com

The text of this books is set in Adobe Garamond Pro
Book design by Susanna Vagt

Library of Congress Cataloging-in-Publication Data is on file.

Manufactured in the United States of America
DOC 10 9
4500525452

3 9957 00186 9557

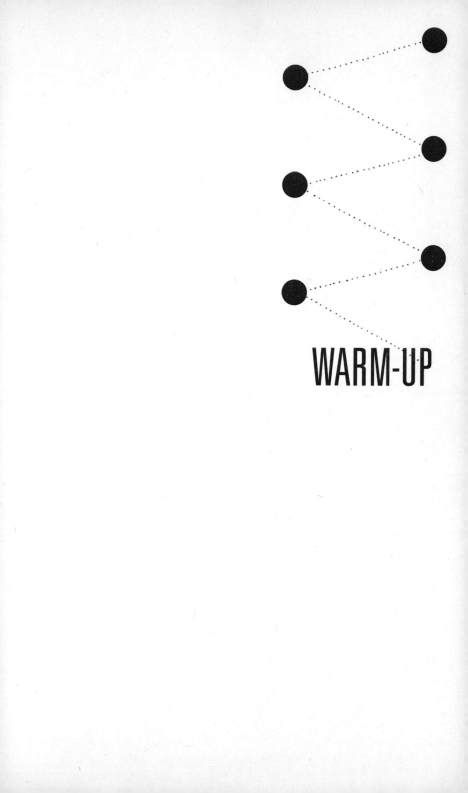

WARM-UP

Dribbling

At the top of the key, I'm
  MOVING & GROOVING,
POPping and *ROCKING*—
Why you BUMPING?
  Why you LOCKING?
Man, take this THUMPING.
Be careful though,
'cause now I'm CRUNKing
  *Criss*CROSSING
FLOSSING
flipping
and my dipping will leave you
S
  L
    I
      P
        P
          I
            N
              G   on the floor, while I
SWOOP in
to the *finish* with a *fierce finger* roll . . .
Straight in the hole:
Swoooooooooooosh.

Josh Bell

is my name.
But *Filthy McNasty* is my claim to fame.
Folks call me that
'cause my game's acclaimed,
so downright dirty, it'll put you to shame.
My hair is long, my height's tall.
See, I'm the next Kevin Durant,
LeBron, and Chris Paul.

Remember the greats,
my dad likes to gloat:
I balled with Magic and the Goat.
But tricks are for kids, I reply.
Don't need your pets
my game's so
fly.

Mom says,
Your dad's old school,
like an ol' Chevette.
You're fresh and new,
like a red Corvette.
Your game so sweet, it's a crêpes suzette.
Each time you play
it's ALLLLLLLLLLLLLLL net.

4

If anyone else called me
fresh and *sweet,*
I'd burn mad as a flame.
But I know she's only talking about my game.
See, when I play ball,
I'm on fire.
When I shoot,
I inspire.
The hoop's for sale,
and I'm the buyer.

How I Got My Nickname

I'm not that big on jazz music, but Dad is.
One day we were listening to a CD
of a musician named Horace Silver, and Dad says,

Josh, this cat is the real deal.
Listen to that piano, fast and free,
Just like you and JB on the court.

It's okay, I guess, Dad.
Okay? DID YOU SAY OKAY?
Boy, you better recognize

greatness when you hear it.
Horace Silver is one of the hippest.
If you shoot half as good as he jams—

Dad, no one says "hippest" anymore.
Well, they ought to, 'cause this cat
is so hip, when he sits down he's still standing, he says.

Real funny, Dad.
You know what, Josh?
What, Dad?

I'm dedicating this next song to you.
What's the next song?
Only the best song,
the funkiest song
on Silver's Paris Blues *album:*
"FILTHY
         McNASTY."

1

At first

I didn't like
the name
because so many kids
made fun of me
on the school bus,
at lunch, in the bathroom.
Even Mom had jokes.

It fits you perfectly, Josh, she said:
You never clean your closet, and
that bed of yours is always filled
with cookie crumbs and candy wrappers.
It's just plain nasty, son.

But, as I got older
and started getting game,
the name took on a new meaning.
And even though I wasn't into
all that jazz,
every time I'd score,
rebound,
or steal a ball,
Dad would jump up
smiling and screamin',

That's my boy out there.
Keep it funky, Filthy!

And that made me feel
real good
about my nickname.

Filthy McNasty

is a MYTHical MANchild
Of rather *dubious distinction*
Always AGITATING
                COMBINATING
and ELEVATING   his game
He   dribbles
          fakes
then   *takes*
the ROCK to the
glass, fast, and on BLAST
But watch out when he shoots
or you'll get SCHOOLed
                FOOLed
                        UNCOOLed
'Cause when FILTHY gets hot
He has a *SLAMMERIFIC SHOT*
It's
Dunkalicious CLASSY
Supersonic SASSY
and   D
          O
          W
          N right
                in your face
mcNASTY

Jordan Bell

My twin brother is a baller.
The only thing he loves
more than basketball
is betting. If it's ninety degrees
outside and the sky is cloudless,
he will bet you
that it's going to rain.
It's annoying
and sometimes
funny.

Jordan insists that everyone
call him *JB*. His favorite player is
Michael Jordan, but he
doesn't want people to think
he's sweating him.
Even though he is.

Evidence: He has one pair
of Air Jordan sneakers
for every month
of the year
including Air Jordan 1 Low
Barack Obama Limited Editions,
which he never wears.

Plus he has MJ sheets, pillowcases,
slippers, socks, underwear, notebooks,
pencils, cups, hats, wristbands,
and sunglasses.

With the fifty dollars he won from a bet
he and Dad made over whether
the Krispy Kreme Hot sign was on (it wasn't)
he purchased
a Michael Jordan toothbrush
("Only used once!") on eBay.
He's right, he's not sweating him.
HE'S STALKING HIM.

On the way to the game

I'm banished to the back
seat with JB,
who only stops
playing with my locks
when I slap him
across his bald head
with my jockstrap.

Five Reasons I Have Locks

5. Some of my favorite rappers have them:
Lil Wayne, 2 Chainz, and Wale.

4. They make me feel
like a king.

3. No one else
on the team has them, and

2. it helps people know
that I am me and not JB.

But
mostly because

1. ever since I watched
the clip of Dad
posterizing
that seven-foot Croatian center
on ESPN's *Best Dunks Ever;*
soaring through the air — his
long twisted hair like wings
carrying him
high above

the rim—I knew
one day
I'd need
my own wings
to fly.

Mom tells Dad

that he has to sit
in the top row
of the bleachers
during the game.

You're too confrontational, she says.

*Filthy, don't forget to
follow through
on your jump shot,*
Dad tells me.

JB tells Mom,
*We're almost in high school,
so no hugs before the game, please.*

Dad says, *You boys
ought to treasure your mother's love.
My mom was like gold to me.*

*Yeah, but your mom
didn't come to ALL
of your games,* JB says.

And she wasn't the assistant school principal either,
I add.

Conversation

Dad, do you miss playing basketball? I ask.
Like jazz misses Dizzy, he says.

Huh?
Like hip-hop misses Tupac, Filthy, he says.

Oh! But you're still young,
you could probably still play, right?

My playing days are over, son.
My job now is to take care of this family.

Don't you get bored sitting
around the house all day?

You could get a job or something.
Filthy, what's all this talk about a job?

You don't think your ol' man knows
how to handle his business?

Boy, I saved my basketball money—
this family is fine. Yeah, I miss

basketball A LOT, and
I do have some feelers out there

about coaching. But honestly,
right now I'm fine coaching this house

and keeping up with you and your brother.
Now go get JB so we won't be late

to the game and Coach benches you.
Why don't you ever wear your championship ring?

Is this Jeopardy *or something? What's with the questions?*
Yeah, I wear it, when I want to floss. Dad smiles.

Can I wear it to school once?
Can you bounce a ball on the roof, off a tree, in the hoop?

Uh . . . no.
Then, I guess you're not Da Man. Only Da Man wears Da
    Ring.

Aw, come on, Dad.
Tell you what: You bring home the trophy this year, and
    we'll see.

Thanks, Dad. You know, if you get bored
you could always write a book, like Vondie's mom did.

She wrote one about spaceships.
A book? What would you have me write about?

Maybe a book of those rules
you give me and JB

before each of our games.
"I'm Da Man" by Chuck Bell, Dad laughs.

That's lame, Dad, I say.
Who you calling lame? Dad says, headlocking me.

Dad, tell me again why they called you Da Man?
Filthy, back in the day, I was the boss, never lost,

I had the sickest double cross, and I kissed
so many pretty ladies, they called me Lip-Gloss.

Oh, really? Mom says, sneaking up on us
like she always seems to do.

Yeah, you *Da Man,* Dad, I laugh,
then throw my gym bag in the trunk.

Basketball Rule #1

In this game of life
your family is the court
and the ball is your heart.
No matter how good you are,
no matter how down you get,
always leave
your heart
on the court.

FIRST QUARTER

JB and I

are almost thirteen. Twins. Two basketball goals at
opposite ends of the court. Identical.
It's easy to tell us apart though. I'm

an inch taller, with dreads to my neck. He gets
his head shaved once a month. I want to go to Duke,
he flaunts Carolina Blue. If we didn't love each other,

we'd HATE each other. He's a shooting guard.
I play forward. JB's the second
most phenomenal baller on our team.

He has the better jumper, but I'm the better
slasher. And much faster. We both
pass well. Especially to each other.

To get ready for the season, I went
to three summer camps. JB only went to
one. Said he didn't want to miss Bible school.

What does he think, I'm stupid? Ever since
Kim Bazemore kissed him in Sunday school,
he's been acting all religious,

thinking less and less about
basketball, and more and more about
GIRLS.

At the End of Warm-Ups,
My Brother Tries to Dunk

Not even close, JB.
What's the matter?
The hoop too high for you? I snicker
but it's not funny to him,
especially when I take off from center court,
my hair like wings,
each lock lifting me higher and HIGHER
like a 747 ZOOM ZOOM!
I throw down so hard,
the fiberglass trembles.
BOO YAH, Dad screams
from the top row.
I'm the only kid
on the team
who can do that.

The gym is a loud, crowded circus.
My stomach is a roller coaster.
My head, a carousel.
The air, heavy with the smell
of sweat, popcorn,
and the sweet perfume
of mothers watching sons.

Our mom, a.k.a. Dr. Bell, a.k.a. The Assistant Principal,
is talking to some of the teachers
on the other side of the gym.
I'm feeling better already.
Coach calls us in,
does his Phil Jackson impersonation.
Love ignites the spirit, brings teams together, he says.
JB and I glance at each other,
ready to bust out laughing,
but Vondie, our best friend,
beats us to it.
The whistle goes off.
Players gather at center circle,
dap each other,
pound each other.
Referee tosses the jump ball.
Game on.

The Sportscaster

JB likes to taunt and
trash talk
during games
like Dad
used to do
when he played.

When I walk onto
the court
I prefer silence
so I can
Watch
React
Surprise.

I talk too,
but mostly
to myself,
like sometimes
when I do
my own
play-by-play
in my head.

Josh's Play-by-Play

It's game three for the two-and-oh Wildcats.
Number seventeen, Vondie Little, grabs it.
Nothing *little* about that kid.
The Wildcats have it,
first play of the game.
The hopes are high tonight at
Reggie Lewis Junior High.
We destroyed Hoover Middle
last week, thirty-two to four,
and we won't stop,
can't stop,
till we claim the championship trophy.
Vondie overhead passes me.
I fling a quick chest pass to my twin brother, JB,
number twenty-three, a.k.a. the Jumper.
I've seen him launch it from thirty feet before,
ALL NET.
That boy is special, and it doesn't hurt
that Chuck "Da Man" Bell is his father.
And mine, too.
JB bounces the ball back to me.
JB's a shooter, but I'm sneaky
and silky as a snake—
and you thought my hair was long.
I'm six feet, all legs.

OH, WOW—DID YOU SEE THAT NASTY CROSS-
OVER?
Now you see why they call me Filthy.
Folks, I hope you got your tickets,
because I'm about to put on a show.

28

cross·o·ver

[KRAWS-OH-VER] *noun*

A simple basketball move
in which a player dribbles
the ball quickly
from one hand
to the other.

As in: When done right,
a *crossover* can break
an opponent's ankles.

As in: Deron Williams's *crossover*
is nice, but Allen Iverson's *crossover*
was so deadly, he could've set up
his own podiatry practice.

As in: Dad taught me
how to give a soft cross first
to see if your opponent falls
for it,
then hit 'em
with the hard *crossover*.

The Show

A *quick* shoulder SHAKE,

a *slick* eye FAKE —

Number 28 is   way past late.

He's reading me like a

BOOK

but I turn the page

and watch him look,

which can only mean I got him

SHOOK.

His feet are the bank

and I'm the *crook.*

Breaking, Braking,

taking him to the left—

now he's took.

Number 14 joins in . . .

Now he's on the   H

                                          O

                                              O

                                                  K

I got TWO in my kitchen

and I'm fixing to **COOK.**

Preppin' my meal, ready for glass . . .
Nobody's expecting Filthy to p a s s
I see Vondie under the hoop
so I serve him up my

Alley-oop.

The Bet, Part One

We're down by seven
at halftime.
Trouble owns our faces
but Coach isn't worried.
Says we haven't found our rhythm yet.
Then, all of a sudden, out of nowhere
Vondie starts dancing the Snake,
only he looks like a seal.
Then Coach blasts his favorite dance music,
and before you know it

we're all doing the Cha-Cha Slide:

>*To the left, take it back now, y'all.*
>
>*One hop this time, right foot, let's stomp.*

JB high-fives me, with a familiar look.
You want to bet, don't you? I ask.
Yep, he says,
then touches
my hair.

Ode to My Hair

If my hair were a tree
I'd climb it.

I'd kneel down beneath
and enshrine it.

I'd treat it like gold
and then mine it.

Each day before school
I unwind it.

And right before games
I entwine it.

These locks on my head,
I designed it.

And one last thing if
you don't mind it:

That bet you just made?
I DECLINE IT.

The Bet, Part Two

IF. I. LOSE.
THE. BET.
YOU. WANT. TO.
WHAT?

If *the score gets tied,* he says, *and*
if *it comes down to the last shot,* he says, *and*
if *I get the ball,* he says, *and*
if *I don't miss,* he says,
I get to cut off
your hair.

Sure, I say, as serious
as a heart attack.
You can cut my locks off,
but if I win the bet
you have to walk around
with no pants on
and no underwear
tomorrow
in school
during lunch.

Vondie
and the rest
of the fellas
laugh like hyenas.

Not to be outdone,
JB revises the bet:
Okay, he says.
How about if you lose
I cut one lock
and if you win
I will moon
that nerdy group
of sixth-graders
that sit
near our table
at lunch?

Even though I used to be one of those nerdy sixth-graders,
even though I love my hair the way Dad loves Krispy Kreme,
even though I don't want us to lose the game,
odds are this is one of JB's legendary bets I'll win,
because
that's a lot of *ifs*.

The game is tied

when JB's soft jumper sails
tick
through the air.
tock
The crowd stills,
tick
mouths drop,
tock
and when his last-second shot
tick

hits net,
tock
the clock stops.
The gym explodes.
Its hard bleachers
empty
and my head
aches.

In the locker room

after the game,
JB cackles like a crow.
He walks up to me
grinning,
holds his hand out
so I can see
the red scissors from Coach's desk
smiling at me, their
steel blades sharp
and ready.

I love this game
like the winter loves snow
even though I spent
the final quarter
in foul trouble
on the bench.
JB was on fire
and we won
and I lost
the bet.

Cut

Time to pay up, Filthy, JB says,
laughing
and waving
the scissors
in the air
like a flag.
My teammates gather around
to salute.
FILTHY, FILTHY, FILTHY, they chant.

He opens the scissors,
grabs my hair
to slash a strand.

I don't hear
my golden lock
hit the floor,
but I do hear
the sound
of calamity
when Vondie
hollers,
OH, SNAP!

ca·lam·i·ty

[KUH-LAM-IH-TEE] *noun*

An unexpected,
undesirable event;
often physically injurious.

As in: If JB hadn't been acting
so silly and
playing around,
he would have cut
one lock
instead of five
from my head
and avoided
this *calamity.*

As in: The HUGE bald patch
on the side
of my head
is a dreadful
calamity.

As in: After the game
Mom almost has a fit
When she sees my hair,

39

What a calamity, she says,
shaking her head
and telling Dad to take me
to the barber shop
on Saturday
to have the rest
cut off.

Mom doesn't like us eating out

but once a month she lets
one of us choose a restaurant
and even though she won't let him touch
half the things on the buffet,
it's Dad's turn
and he chooses Chinese.
I know what he really wants
is Pollard's Chicken and BBQ,
but Mom has banned
us from that place.

In the Golden Dragon,
Mom is still frowning
at JB for messing up my hair.
But, Mom, it was an accident, he says.
*Accident or not, you owe
your brother an apology,* she tells him.

I'm sorry for cutting your filthy hair, Filthy, JB laughs.
Not so funny now, is it? I say, my knuckles
digging into his scalp
till Dad saves him from the noogie
with one of his lame jokes:

Why can't you play sports in the jungle? he asks.

Mom repeats the question because
Dad won't continue until someone does.
Because of the cheetahs, he snaps back,
so amused, he almost falls out of his chair,
which causes all of us to laugh, and
get past my hair issue
for now.

I fill my plate with egg rolls and dumplings.
JB asks Dad how we did.
Y'all did okay, Dad says, *but, JB, why did you
let that kid post you up? And, Filthy,
what was up with that lazy crossover?
When I was playing, we never . . .*

And while Dad is telling us another story
for the hundredth time, Mom removes the salt
from the table and JB goes to the buffet.
He brings back three packages
of duck sauce and a cup of wonton soup
and hands them all to me.
Dad pauses, and Mom looks at JB.
That was random, she says.
What, isn't that what you wanted, Filthy? JB asks.
And even though I never opened my mouth,
I say, Thanks,
because
it is.

Missing

I am not
a mathematician—
$a + b$ seldom
equals c.
Pluses and minuses,
we get along
but we are not close.
I am no Pythagoras.

And so each time
I count the locks
of hair
beneath my pillow
I end up with thirty-seven
plus one tear,
which never
adds up.

The inside of Mom and Dad's bedroom closet

is off-limits,
so every time JB asks me
to go in there to look
through Dad's stuff, I say no.
But today when I ask Mom
for a box to put my dreadlocks in,
she tells me to take
one of her Sunday hat boxes
from the top shelf
of her closet.

Next to her purple hat box is
Dad's small silver safety box
with the key in the lock
and practically begging me
to open it,
so I do, when, unexpectedly:
What are you doing, Filthy?
Standing in the doorway
is JB with a look that says BUSTED!
Filthy, you still giving me the silent treatment?
. . .
I really am sorry about your hair, man.
I owe you, Filthy, so I'm gonna cut
the grass for the rest of the year and

pick up the leaves . . . and I'll wash the cars
and I'll even wash your hair.
Oh, you got jokes, huh? I say, then grab him
and give him another noogie.

So, what are you doing in here, Filthy?

Nothing, Mom said I could use her hat box.
That doesn't look like a hat box, Filthy.
Let me see that, he says.

And just like that
we're rummaging through
a box filled with newspaper clippings
about Chuck "Da Man" Bell
and torn ticket stubs
and old flyers
and . . .

WHOA! There it is, Filthy, JB says.
And even though we've seen Dad
wear it many times, actually holding
his glossy championship ring
in our hands
is more than magical.
Let's try it on, I whisper.
But JB is a step ahead, already sliding
it on each of his fingers

until he finds one it fits.
What else is in there, JB? I ask,
hoping he will realize it's my turn
to wear Dad's championship ring.

There's a bunch of articles about
Dad's triple-doubles, three-point records,
and the time he made fifty free throws
in a row at the Olympic finals, he says,
finally handing me the ring,
and an Italian article
about Dad's *bellissimo* crossover
and his million-dollar multiyear contract
with the European league.

We already know all this stuff, JB.
Anything new, or secret-type stuff? I ask.
And then JB pulls out a manila envelope.
I grab it, glance at the PRIVATE
stamped on the front.
In the moment
that I decide to put it back,
JB snatches it.
Let's do this, he says.
I resist, ready to take
the purple hat box
and jet,

but I guess the mystery
is just too much.

We open it. There are two letters.
The first letter reads:
Chuck Bell, the Los Angeles Lakers would like to
invite you to our free-agent tryouts.
We open the other. It starts:
Your decision not to have surgery
means that realistically,
with patella tendonitis,
you may not be able to play

again.   47

pa·tel·la ten·di·ni·tis

[PUH-TEL-UH TEN-DUH-NAHY-TIS] *noun*

The condition
that arises when the muscle
that connects the kneecap
to the shin bone
becomes irritated
due to overuse,
especially from jumping activities.

As in: On the top shelf
of Mom and Dad's closet
in a silver safety box
JB and I discovered
that my dad has jumper's knee,
a.k.a. *patella tendonitis.*

As in: As a rookie,
my dad led his team
to the Euroleague championship,
but thanks to *patella tendonitis,*
he went from a superstar
with a million-dollar fadeaway jumper

to a star
whose career
had faded away.

As in: I wonder why my dad
never had surgery
on his *patella tendonitis.*

Sundays After Church

When the prayers end
and the doors open
the Bells hit center stage
and the curtain opens up on
the afternoon pick-up game
in the gym
at the county recreation center.
The cast is full of regulars
and rookies
with cartoon names like
FlapJack,
Scoobs,
and Cookie.
The hip-hop soundtrack blasts.
The bass booms.
The crowd looms.
There's music and mocking,
teasing nonstop, but
when the play begins
all the talk ceases.
Dad shovel-passes the ball to me.
I behind-the-back pass to JB,
who sinks a twenty-foot three.
See, this is how we act
Sundays after church.

Basketball Rule #2

(Random text from Dad)

Hustle dig
Grind push
Run fast
Change pivot
Chase pull
Aim shoot
Work smart
Live smarter
Play hard
Practice harder

Girls

I walk into the lunchroom with JB.
Heads turn.
I'm not bald like JB,
but my hair's close enough
so that people sprinting past us
do double-takes.
Finally, after we sit at our table,
the questions come:
Why'd you cut your hair, Filthy?
How can we tell who's who?
JB answers, *I'm the cool one*
who makes free throws,
and I holler,
I'M THE ONE WHO CAN DUNK.
We both get laughs.
Some girl who we've never seen before,
in tight jeans and pink Reeboks,
comes up to the table.
JB's eyes are ocean wide,
his mouth swimming on the floor,
his clownish grin, embarrassing.
So when she says,

Is it true that twins
know what each other are thinking?
I tell her
you don't have to be his *twin*
to know
what *he's* thinking.

While Vondie and JB

debate whether the new girl
is a knockout or just beautiful,
a hottie or a cutie,
a lay-up or a dunk,
I finish my vocabulary homework—
and my brother's vocabulary homework,
which I don't mind
since English is my favorite subject
and he did the dishes for me last week.
But it's hard to concentrate
in the lunchroom
with the girls' step team
practicing in one corner,
a rap group performing in the other,
and Vondie and JB
waxing poetic
about love and basketball.
So when they ask,
What do you think, Filthy?
I tell 'em,
She's pulchritudinous.

pul·chri·tu·di·nous

[PALL-KRE-TOO-DEN-NUS] *adjective*

Having great physical
beauty and appeal.

As in: Every guy
in the lunchroom
is trying to flirt
with the new girl
because she's so *pulchritudinous.*

As in: I've never had a girlfriend,
but if I did, you better believe
she'd be *pulchritudinous.*

As in: Wait a minute—
why is the *pulchritudinous* new girl
now talking
to my brother?

Practice

Coach reads to us from
The Art of War:
A winning strategy is
not about planning, he says.
It's about quick responses
to changing conditions.
Then he has us do
footwork drills
followed by
forty wind sprints
from the baseline
to half court.
The winner doesn't
have to practice today, Coach says,
and Vondie blasts off
like *Apollo 17,*
his long legs
giving him an edge,
but I'm the quickest guy
on the team,
so on the last lap
I run hard,

take the lead by a foot,
and even though I don't plan it,
I let him win
and get ready to practice
harder.

Walking Home

Hey, JB, you think we can win
the county championship this year?
I don't know, man.
Hey, JB, why do you think
Dad never had
knee surgery?
Man, I don't know.
Hey, JB, why can't Dad eat—
Look, Filthy, we'll win
if you stop missing free throws.
Nobody likes doctors.
And Dad can't eat foods with too much salt
because Mom told him he can't.
Any more questions?
Yeah, one more.
You want to play
to twenty-one
when we get home?
Sure. You got ten dollars? he asks.

Man to Man

In the driveway, I'm
        SHAKING AND BAKING.
You don't want none of this, I say.
I'm about to TAKE ɪᴛ TO ᴛʜᴇ HOLE.
Keep your eye on the ball.
I'd hate to see you
F
A
L
L
You shoulda gone with your GIRLFRIEND
to the mall.
Just play ball, JB shouts.
Okay, but WATCH OUT, my BROTHER,
TARHEEL LOVER.
I'm about to go **UNDER**
             COVER.
Then bring it, he says.
And I do, all the way to the top.
So SMOOOOOOOOTH, I make him
      drop.
So *nasty,* the floor should be mopped.
But before I can shoot,
Mom makes us stop:

Josh, come clean your room!

After dinner

Dad takes us
to the Rec
to practice
shooting free throws
with one hand
while he stands
two feet in front
of us,
waving frantically
in our faces.

It will teach you focus, he reminds us.

Three players
from the local college
recognize Dad
and ask him
for autographs
       "for our parents."
Dad chuckles
along with them.
JB ignores them.
I challenge them:

It won't be so funny
when we shut
you amateurs down,
will it? I say.
OHHHH, this young boy got hops
like his ol' man? the tallest one says.
Talk is cheap, Dad says. *If y'all want to run,*
let's do this. First one to eleven.
The tall one asks Dad if he needs crutches,
then checks the ball to me,
and the game begins,
right after JB screams:

Loser pays twenty bucks!

After we win

I see the pink
Reeboks–wearing girl
shooting baskets
on the other court.
She plays ball, too?
JB walks over to her
and I can tell
he likes her
because when she goes in
for a lay-up,
he doesn't slap
the ball silly
like he tries
to do with me.
He just stands there
looking silly,
smiling
on the other court
at the pink
Reeboks–wearing girl.

Dad Takes Us to Krispy Kreme and Tells Us His Favorite Story (Again)

Didn't Mom say no more doughnuts? JB asks Dad.
What your mother doesn't know
won't hurt her, he answers, biting
into his third chocolate glazed cruller.
Good shooting today. We beat
those boys like they stole something, he adds.
Why didn't we take their money, Dad? I ask.
They were kids, Filthy, just like y'all.
The look on their faces
after we beat them
eleven to nothing
was enough for me.

Remember
when you were two
and I taught you the game?
You had a bottle in one hand
and a ball in the other,
and your mom thought I was crazy.
I WAS crazy.
Crazy in love.
With my twin boys.

Once, when you were three,
I took you to the park
to shoot free throws.
The guy who worked there said,
"This basket is ten feet tall.
For older kids. Kids like yours
might as well shoot
at the sun." And then he laughed.
And I asked him if a deaf person
could write music. And he said,
"Huh?" then
took out his wrench and told me,
"I'm gonna lower the goal for y'all."

We remember, Dad.
And then you told us Beethoven
was a famous musician who was deaf,
and how many times do we have to hear
the same—
And
Dad interrupts me:
Interrupt me again and I'll start all over.
Like I was saying,
I handed both of you a ball.
Stood you between the foul line
and the rim. Told you to shoot.

You did. And it was musical. Like
the opening of Beethoven's Fifth.
Da da da duhhhhhhhhhh. Da da da duuuuuuuuuuh.
Your shots whistled. Like a train
pulling into the station. I expected
you to make it. And you did.
The guy was in shock.
He looked at me
like
he'd missed
the train.

Basketball Rule #3

Never let anyone
lower your goals.
Others' expectations
of you are determined
by their limitations
of life.
The sky is your limit, sons.
Always shoot
for the sun
and you *will* shine.

Josh's Play-by-Play

The Red Rockets,
defending county champions,
are in the house tonight.
They brought their whole school.
This place is oozing crimson.
They're beating us
twenty-nine to twenty-eight
with less than a minute to go.
I'm at the free-throw line.
All I have to do
is make both shots
to take the lead.
The first is up, UP, and—
CLANK!—it hits the rim.
The second looks . . . real . . . goo . . .
MISSED AGAIN!
But
Vondie grabs the rebound,
a fresh twenty-four on the shot clock.
Number thirty-three on the Rockets
strips the ball from Vondie.
This game is like Ping-Pong,
with all the back-and-forth.
He races downcourt
for an easy lay —

OHHHHHHH!

Houston, we have a problem!

I catch him

and slap

the ball on the glass.

Ever seen anything like this from a seventh-grader?

Didn't think so!

Me and JB are stars in the making.

The Rockets full-court-press me.

But I get it across the line just in time.

Ten seconds left.

I pass the ball to JB.

They double-team him in a hurry—don't want to give

him an easy three.

Five seconds left.

JB lobs the ball,

I rise like a Learjet—

seventh-graders aren't supposed to dunk.

But guess what?

I snatch the ball out of the air and

SLAM!

YAM! IN YOUR MUG!

Who's *Da Man?*

Let's look at that again.

Oh, I forgot, this is junior high.

No instant replay until college.

Well, with game like this

that's where me and JB

are headed.

The new girl

comes up to me
after the game,
her smile ocean wide
my mouth wide shut.
Nice dunk, she says.
Thanks.
Y'all coming to the gym
over the Thanksgiving break?
Probably!
Cool. By the way, why'd you cut your locks?
They were kind of cute.
Standing right behind me, Vondie giggles.
Kind of cute, he mocks.

Then JB walks up.

Hey, JB, great game.
I brought you some iced tea, she says.
Is it sweet? he asks.
And just like that
JB and the new girl
are sipping sweet tea
together.

I Missed Three Free Throws Tonight

Each night
after dinner
Dad makes us
shoot
free throws
until we make ten
in a row.

Tonight he says
I have to make
fifteen.

Basketball Rule #4

If you miss
enough of life's
free throws
you will pay
in the end.

Having a mother

is good when she rescues you
from free-throw attempt number thirty-six,
your arms as heavy as sea anchors.
But it can be bad
when your mother
is a principal at your school.
Bad in so many ways.
It's always *education*
this and *education that*.

72

After a double-overtime
basketball game I only want
three things: food, bath, sleep.
The last thing I want is EDUCATION!
But, each night,
Mom makes us read.
Don't know how he does it, but
JB listens to his iPod
at the same time,
so he doesn't hear me
when I ask him
is Miss Sweet Tea his girlfriend.

He claims he's listening to French classical,

that it helps him concentrate.

Yeah, right! Sounds more like

Jay-Z and Kanye

in Paris.

Which is why when Mom and Dad start arguing,

he doesn't hear them, either.

Mom shouts

Get a checkup. Hypertension is genetic.
I'm fine, stop high-posting me, baby, Dad whispers.

Don't play me, Charles—this isn't a basketball game.
I don't need a doctor, I'm fine.

Your father didn't "need" a doctor either.
He was alive when he went into the hospital.

So now you're afraid of hospitals?
Nobody's afraid. I'm fine. It's not that serious.

Fainting is a joke, is it?
I saw you, baby, and I got a little excited. Come kiss me.

Don't do that . . .
Baby, it's nothing. I just got a little dizzy.

You love me?
Like summer loves short nights.

Get a checkup, then.
Only cure I need is you.

I'm serious about this, Chuck.

Only doctor I need is Dr. Crystal Bell. Now come
here . . .

And then there is silence, so I put the pillow over my
head
because when they stop talking,

I know what that means.
Uggghh!

hy·per·ten·sion

[HI-PER-TEN-SHUHN] *noun*

A disease
otherwise known as
high blood pressure.

As in: Mom doesn't want Dad
eating salt, because too much of it
increases the volume
of blood,
which can cause *hypertension*.

As in: *Hypertension*
can affect all types of people,
but you have a higher risk
if someone in your family
has had the disease.

As in: I think
my grandfather
died of *hypertension*?

To fall asleep

I count
and recount
the thirty-seven strands
of my past
in the box
beneath my bed.

Why We Only Ate Salad for Thanksgiving

Because every year
Grandma makes
a big delicious dinner
but this year
two days before
Thanksgiving
she fell off
her front stoop
on the way
to buy groceries

so Uncle Bob
my mom's younger brother
    (who smokes cigars
    and thinks he's a chef
    because he watches
    Food TV)
decided he would
prepare a feast
for the whole family
which consisted of
macaroni with no cheese
concrete-hard cornbread
and a greenish-looking ham
that prompted Mom

to ask if he had any eggs
to go along with it
which made grandma laugh so hard
she fell again, this time
right out of her wheelchair.

How Do You Spell Trouble?

During the vocabulary test
JB passes me a folded note
to give to
Miss Sweet Tea,
who sits at the desk
in front of me
and who looks
pretty tight
in her pink denim capris
and matching sneaks.

Someone cracks a window.
A cold breeze whistles.
Her hair dances to its own song.
In this moment I forget
about the test
and the note
until JB hits me in the head with his No. 2.

Somewhere between
camaraderie and *imbecile*
I tap her beige bare shoulder
with the note.

At that exact moment
the teacher's head creeps
up from his desk, his eyes directly on me.

I'm a fly caught in a web.
What do I do?
Hand over the note, embarrass JB;
or hide the note, take the heat.
I look at my brother,
his forehead a factory of sweat.
Miss Sweet Tea smiles,
gorgeous pink lips and all.

I know what I have to do.   81

Bad News

I sit in Mom's office
for an hour,
reading
brochures and pamphlets
about the Air Force and the Marines.

She's in and out
handling principal stuff:
a parent protesting her daughter's F;
a pranked substitute teacher crying;
a broken window.

After an hour
she finally sits
in the chair next to me
and says, *The good news is,*
I'm not going to suspend you.

The bad news, Josh,
is that
neither Duke nor any other college
accepts cheaters. Since I can't
seem to make a decent man out of you
perhaps the Air Force or Marines can.

I want to tell her I wasn't cheating,
that this is all JB and Miss Sweet Tea's fault,
that this will never happen again,
that Duke is the only thing that matters,
but a water pipe bursts in the girls' bathroom.

So I tell her I'm sorry,
it won't happen again,
then head off to my next class.

Gym class

is supposed to be about balls:
volleyballs, basketballs, softballs,
soccer balls—sometimes sit-ups
and always sweat.

But today Mr. Lane tells
us not to dress out.
He's standing in front of the class,
a dummy laid out on the floor,

plastic, faceless, torso cut in half.
I'm not paying attention
to anything he's saying
or to the dummy

because
I'm watching Jordan pass notes
to Miss Sweet Tea. And I
wonder what's in the notes.

Josh, why don't you come up
and assist me.
What? Huh?
The class snickers,

and before I know it
I'm tilting the dummy's head back,
pinching his nose,
blowing in his mouth,

and pumping his chest
thirty times.
All the while
thinking that if life is really fair

one day I'll be the one
writing notes to some sweet girl
and JB will have to squash his lips
on some dummy's sweaty mouth.

SECOND QUARTER

Conversation

Hey, JB,
I played a pickup game
at the Rec today.
At first, the older guys laughed
and wouldn't let me in
unless I could hit from half-court . . .

Of course, I did. All net.

I wait for JB to say something,
but he just smiles,
his eyes all moony.

I showed them guys
how the Bells ball.
I scored fourteen points.
They told me I should
try out for junior varsity next year
'cause I got hops . . .

JB, are you listening?

JB nods, his fingers tapping away
on the computer, chatting
probably with
Miss Sweet Tea.

I told the big guys about you, too.
They said we could come back and
run with them anytime.
What do you think about that?

HELLO—Earth to JB?

Even though I know he hears me,
the only thing JB is listening to
is the sound of his heart
bouncing
on the court
of love.

Conversation

Dad, this girl is making
Jordan act weird.
He's here, but he's not.
He's always smiling.
His eyes get all spacey
whenever she's around,
and sometimes when she's not.
He wears your cologne.
He's always
texting her.
He even wore loafers to school.
Dad, you gotta do something.

Dad does *something.*
He laughs.

Filthy, talking to your brother
right now
would be like pushing water uphill
with a rake, son.

This isn't funny, Dad.
Say something
to him. Please.

Filthy, if some girl
done locked up JB,
he's going to jail.
Now let's go get some doughnuts.

Basketball Rule #5

When
you stop
playing
your game
you've already
lost.

Showoff

UP by sixteen
with *six seconds*
showing, JB smiles,
then STRUTS
side
    steps
        stutters
Spins, and
S
I
N
K
S
a sick SLICK SLIDING
sweeeeeeeeeeT
SEVEN-foot shot.

What a showoff.

Out of Control

Are you kidding me?
Come on. Ref, open your eyes.
Ray Charles could have seen
that kid walked.
CALL THE TRAVELING VIOLATION!
You guys are TERRIBLE!

Mom wasn't
at the game
tonight,
which meant
that all night
Dad was free
to yell
at the officials,
which he did.

Mom calls me into the kitchen

after we get home from beating
St. Francis. Normally she wants
me to sample the macaroni and cheese
to make sure it's cheesy enough,
or the oven-baked fried chicken
to make sure it's not greasy and
stuff, but today on the table
is some gross-looking
orange creamy dip with brown specks in it.
A tray of pita-bread triangles is beside it.

Maybe Mom is having one of
her book club meetings.
Sit down, she says. I sit as far
away from the dip as possible.
Maybe the chicken is in the oven.
Where is your brother? she asks.
Probably on the phone with that *girl.*
She hands me a pita.
No thanks, I say, then stand up
to leave, but she gives me a look
that tells me she's not finished
with me. Maybe the mac is in the oven.
We've talked to you two about

your grandfather, she says.
He was a good man. I'm sorry you never got to meet him,
Josh.
Me too, he looked cool in his uniforms.
That man was way past cool.
Dad said he used to curse
a lot and talk about the war.
Mom's laugh is short, then she's serious again.
I know we told
you Grandpop died after a fall, but
the truth is he fell because he had a stroke.
He had a heart disease. Too
many years of bad eating and not taking
care of himself and so —

What does this have
to do with anything? I ask,
even though I think I already know.
Well, our family has a history
of heart problems, she says,
so we're going to start eating better.
Especially Dad. And we're going to
start tonight with
some hummus and
pita bread.
FOR MY VICTORY DINNER?
Josh, we're going to try to lay off the fried foods

and Golden Dragon. And when your dad
takes you to the recreation center,
no Pollard's or Krispy Kreme afterward, understand?
And I understand more than she thinks I do.
But is hummus really the answer?

35–18

is the final score
of game six.
A local reporter
asks JB and I
how we got so good.
Dad screams from behind us,
They learned from Da Man!
The crowd of parents and students
behind us laughs.

On the way home
Dad asks if we should stop
at Pollard's.
I tell him I'm not hungry,
plus I have a lot of homework,
even though
I skipped lunch today
and finished my homework
during halftime.

Too Good

Lately, I've been feeling
like everything in my life
is going right:
I beat JB in *Madden*.
Our team is undefeated.
I scored an A+ on the vocabulary test.
Plus, Mom's away at a conference,
which means
so is the Assistant Principal.

100   I am a little worried, though,
because, as Coach likes to say,
you can get used to
things going well,
but you're never prepared
for something
going wrong.

I'm on Free Throw Number Twenty-Seven

We take turns,
switching every time we miss.
JB has hit forty-one,

the last twelve in a row.
Filthy, keep up, man, keep up, he says.
Dad laughs loud, and says,

Filthy, your brother is putting on
a free-throw clinic. You better—
And suddenly he bowls over,

a look of horror on his face,
and starts coughing
while clutching his chest,

only no sound comes. I freeze.
JB runs over to him.
Dad, you okay? he asks.

I still can't move. There is a stream
of sweat on Dad's face. Maybe
he's overheating, I say.

His mouth is curled up
like a little tunnel. JB grabs
the water hose, turns the

faucet on full blast, and sprays
Dad. Some of it goes in Dad's mouth.
Then I hear the sound

of coughing, and Dad is no longer leaning
against the car, now he's moving
toward the hose, and laughing.

So is JB.
Then Dad grabs the hose
and sprays both of us.

Now I'm laughing too,
but only
on the outside.

He probably

just got something stuck
in his throat,
JB says
when I ask him
if he thought
Dad was sick
and shouldn't we
tell Mom
what happened.

So, when the phone rings,
it's ironic
that after saying hello,
he throws the phone to me,
because, even though
his lips are moving,
JB is speechless,
like he's got something stuck
in his
throat.

i·ron·ic

[AY-RON-IK] *adjective*

Having a curious or humorous
unexpected sequence of events
marked by coincidence.

As in: The fact that Vondie
hates astronomy
and his mom works for NASA
is *ironic.*

As in: It's not *ironic*
that Grandpop died
in a hospital
and Dad doesn't like
doctors.

As in: Isn't it *ironic*
that showoff JB,
with all his swagger,
is too shy
to talk
to Miss Sweet Tea,
so he gives me the phone?

This Is Alexis — May I Please Speak to Jordan?

Identical twins
are no different
from everyone else,
except we look and
sometimes sound
exactly alike.

Phone Conversation (I Sub for JB)

Was that your brother?
Yep, that was Josh. I'm JB.

I know who you are, silly—I called you.
Uh, right. You have any siblings, Alexis?

Two sisters. I'm the youngest.
And the prettiest.

You haven't seen them.
I don't need to.

That's sweet.
Sweet as pomegranate.

Okay, that was random.
That's me.

Jordan, can I ask you something?
Yep.

Did you get my text?
Uh, yeah.

So, what's your answer?
Uh, my answer. I don't know.

Stop being silly, Jordan.
I'm not.

Then tell me your answer. Are y'all rich?
I don't know.

Didn't your dad play in the NBA?
No, he played in Italy.

But still, he made a lot of money, right?
It's not like we're opulent.

Who says "opulent"?
I do.

You never use big words like that at school . . .
I have a reputation to uphold.

Is he cool?
Who?

Your dad.
Very.

So, when are you gonna introduce me?
Introduce you?

To your parents.
I'm waiting for the right moment.

Which is when?
Uh—

So, am I your girlfriend or not?
Uh, can you hold on for a second?

Sure, she says.

Cover the mouthpiece, JB mouths to me.
I do, then whisper to him:

She wants to know are you her boyfriend.
And when are you gonna introduce her

to Mom and Dad. What should I tell her, JB?
Tell her yeah, I guess, I mean, I don't know.

I gotta pee, JB says, running
out of the room, leaving me still in his shoes.

Okay, I'm back, Alexis.
So, what's the verdict, Jordan?

Do you want to be my girlfriend?
Are you asking me to be your girl?

Uh, I think so.
You think so? Well, I have to go now.

Yes.
Yes, what?

I like you. A lot.
I like you, too . . . Precious.

So, now I'm Precious?
Everyone calls you JB.

Then I guess it's official.
Text me later.

Good night, Miss Sweet—
What did you call me?

Uh, good night, my sweetness.
Good night, Precious.

JB comes running out of the bathroom.
What'd she say, Josh? Come on, tell me.

She said she likes me a lot, I tell him.
You mean she likes me *a lot?* he asks.

Yeah . . .
that's what I meant.

JB and I

eat lunch
together
every day,
taking bites
of Mom's
tuna salad
on wheat
between arguments:
Who's the better dunker,
Blake or LeBron?

Which is superior,
Nike
or Converse?
Only today
I wait
at our table
in the back
for twenty-five minutes,
texting Vondie
     (home sick),
eating a fruit cup
     (alone),
before I see

JB strut
into the cafeteria
with Miss Sweet Tea
holding his
precious hand.

Boy walks into a room

with a girl.
They come over.
He says, *Hey, Filthy McNasty*
like he's said forever,
but it sounds different
this time,
and when he snickers,
she does too,
like it's some inside joke,
and my nickname,
some dirty
punch
line.

At practice

Coach says we need to work
on our mental game.
If we *think*
we can beat Independence Junior High —
the defending champions,
the number one seed,
the only other undefeated team —
then we *will*.
But instead of drills
and sprints,
we sit on our butts,
make weird sounds —

       Ohmmmmmmmm Ohmmmmmmmmm —
and meditate.
Suddenly I get this vision
of JB in a hospital.
I quickly open my eyes,
turn around,
and see him looking dead
at me like he's just seen
a ghost.

Second-Person

After practice, you walk home alone.

This feels strange to you, because

as long as you can remember

there has always been a second person.

On today's long, hot mile,

you bounce your basketball,

but your mind

is on something else.

Not whether you will make the playoffs.

Not homework.

Not even what's for dinner.

You wonder what JB

and his pink Reebok–wearing girlfriend are doing.

You do not want to go to the library.

But you go.

Because your report on *The Giver* is due

tomorrow.

And JB has your copy.

But he's with her.

Not here with you.

Which is unfair.

Because he doesn't argue

with you about who's the greatest,

Michael Jordan or Bill Russell,

like he used to.

Because JB will not eat lunch
with you tomorrow
or the next day,
or next week.
Because you are walking home
by yourself
and your brother owns the world.

Third Wheel

You walk into the library,

glance over at the music section.

You look through the magazines.

You even sit at a desk and pretend to study.

You ask the librarian where you can find *The Giver.*

She says something odd:

Did you find your friend?

Then she points upstairs.

On the second floor,

you pass by the computers.

Kids checking their Facebook.

More kids in line waiting

to check their Facebook.

In the Biography section

you see an old man

reading *The Tipping Point.*

You walk down the last aisle,

Teen Fiction,

and come to the reason you're here.

You remove the book

from the shelf.

And there,

behind the last row of books,

you find
the "friend"
the librarian was talking about.
Only she's not your friend
and she's kissing
your brother.

tip·ping point

[TIH-PING POYNT]   *noun*

The point
when an object shifts
from one position
into a new,
entirely different one.

As in: My dad says the *tipping point*
of our country's economy
was housing gamblers
and greedy bankers.

As in: If we get one C
on our report cards,
I'm afraid
Mom will reach
her *tipping point*
and that will be the end
of basketball.

As in: Today at the library,
I went upstairs,

118

walked down an aisle,
pulled *The Giver*
off the shelf,
and found
my *tipping point.*

The main reason I can't sleep

is not because
of the game tomorrow tonight,
is not because
the stubble on my head feels
like bugs are break dancing on it,
is not even because I'm worried about Dad.

The main reason
I can't sleep tonight
is because

Jordan is on the phone
with Miss Sweet Tea
and between the giggling
and the breathing
he tells her
how much she's
the apple of
his eye
and that he wants
to peel her
and get under her skin
and give me a break.

I'm still hungry
and right about now
I wish I had
an apple
of my own.

Surprised

I have it all planned out.
When we walk to the game
I will talk to JB
man to man
about how he's spending
way more time with Alexis
than with me
and Dad.

Except when I hear
the horn,
I look outside
my window and it's raining
and JB is jumping
into a car
with Miss Sweet Tea and her dad,
ruining my plan.

Conversation

In the car
I ask Dad

if going to the doctor
will kill him.

He tells me
he doesn't trust doctors,

that my grandfather did
and look where it got him:

six feet under
at forty-five.

But Mom says your dad
was really sick, I tell him,

and Dad just rolls his eyes,
so I try something different.

I tell him
that just because your teammate

gets fouled on a lay-up
doesn't mean you shouldn't

ever drive to the lane again.
He looks at me and

laughs so loud,
we almost don't hear

the flashing blues
behind us.

124

Game Time: 6:00 p.m.

At 5:28 p.m.
a cop
pulls us over
because Dad has
a broken
taillight.

At 5:30
the officer approaches
our car
and asks Dad
for his driver's license
and registration.

At 5:32
the team leaves
the locker room and
pregame warm-ups
begin
without me.

At 5:34
Dad explains
to the officer
that his license

is in his wallet,
which is in his jacket
at home.

At 5:37
Dad says, *Look, sir,*
my name is Chuck Bell,
and I'm just trying
to get my boy
to his basketball game.

At 5:47
while Coach leads
the Wildcats
in team prayer,
I pray Dad
won't get arrested.

At 5:48
the cop smiles
after verifying
Dad's identity
on Google, and says,
You "Da Man"!

At 5:50
Dad autographs
a Krispy Kreme napkin

for the officer
and gets a warning
for his broken taillight.

At 6:01
we arrive at the game
but on my sprint
into the gym
I slip and fall
in the mud.

This is my second year

playing
for the Reggie Lewis Wildcats
and I've started every game
until tonight,
when Coach tells me
to go get cleaned up
then find a seat
on the bench.

When I try to tell him
it wasn't my fault,
he doesn't want to hear
about sirens and broken taillights.
Josh, better an hour too soon
than a minute too late, he says,
turning his attention back
to JB and the guys
on the court,

all of whom are pointing
and laughing
at me.

Basketball Rule #6

A great team
has a good scorer
with a teammate
who's on point
and ready
to assist.

Josh's Play-by-Play

At the beginning
of the second half
we're up twenty-three to twelve.
I enter the game
for the first time.
I'm just happy
to be back on the floor.
When my brother and I
are on the court together
this team is

unstoppable,
unfadeable.
And, yes,
undefeated.
JB brings the ball up the court.
Passes the ball to Vondie.
He shoots it back to JB.
I call for the ball.
JB finds me in the corner.
I know y'all think
it's time for the pick-and-roll,
but I got something else in mind.
I get the ball on the left side.
JB is setting the pick.
Here it comes—

I roll to his right.
The double-team is on me,
leaving JB free.
He's got his hands in the air,
looking for the dish
from me.
Dad likes to say,
When Jordan Bell is open
you can take his three to the bank,
cash it in, 'cause it's all money.
Tonight, I'm going for broke.
I see JB's still wide open.
McDonald's drive-thru open.
But I got my own plans.
The double-team is still on me
like feathers on a bird.
Ever seen an eagle soar?
So high, so fly.
Me and my wings are—
and that's when I remember:
MY. WINGS. ARE. GONE.
Coach Hawkins is out of his seat.
Dad is on his feet, screaming.
JB's screaming.
The crowd's screaming,
FILTHY, PASS THE BALL!
The shot clock is at 5.
I dribble out of the double-team.

4

Everything comes to a head.

3

I see Jordan.

2

You want it that bad? HERE YA GO!

1 . . .

Before

Today, I walk into the gym
covered in more dirt than a chimney.
When JB screams *FILTHY'S McNasty,*
the whole team laughs. Even Coach.

Then I get benched for the entire first half. For being late.
Today, I watch as we take a big lead,
and JB makes four threes in a row.
I hear the crowd cheer for JB, especially Dad and Mom.

Then I see JB wink at Miss Sweet Tea
after he hits a stupid free throw.
Today, I finally get into the game
at the start of the second half.

JB sets a wicked pick for me
just like Coach showed us in practice,
And I get double-teamed on the roll
just like we expect.

Today, I watch JB get open and wave for me to pass.
Instead I dribble, trying to get out of the trap,
and watch as Coach and Dad scream
for me to pass.

Today, I plan on passing the ball to JB,

but when I hear him say "FILTHY,

give me the ball," I dribble

over to my brother

and fire a pass

so hard,

it levels him,

the blood

from his nose

still shooting

long after the shot-

clock buzzer goes off.

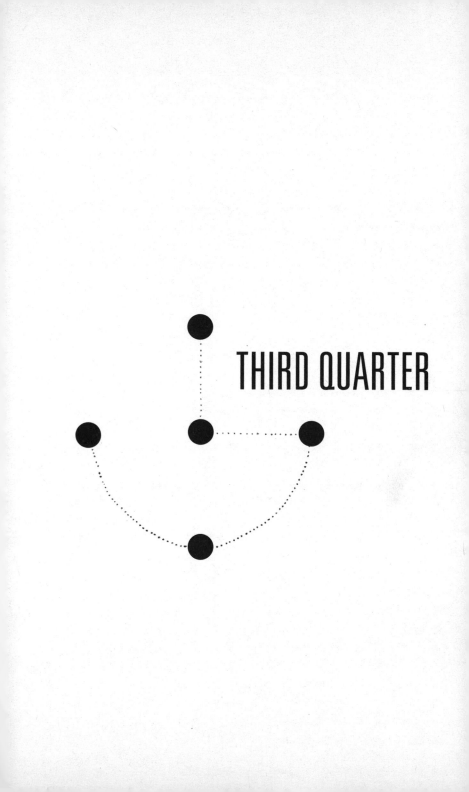

THIRD QUARTER

After

On the short ride home
from the hospital

there is no jazz music
or hoop talk,
only brutal silence,

the unspoken words
volcanic and weighty.
Dad and Mom,
solemn and wounded.

JB, bandaged and hurt,
leans against his back-seat window
and with less than two feet
between us
I feel miles away

from all of them.

Suspension

Sit down, Mom says.
Feels like we're in her office.

Can I make you a sandwich?
But we're in the kitchen.

You want a tall glass of orange soda?
Mom doesn't ever let us drink soda.

Eat up, because this may be your last meal.
Here it comes . . .

Boys with no self-control become men behind bars.
. . .

Have you lost your mind, son?
No.

Did your father and I raise you to be churlish?
No.

So, what's been wrong with you these past few weeks?
. . .

Put that sandwich down and answer me.
I guess I've been just—

You've been just what? DERANGED?
Uh—

DON'T "UH" ME! Talk like you have some sense.
I didn't mean to hurt him.

You could have permanently injured your brother.
I know. I'm sorry, Mom.

You're sorry for what?
. . .

I'm confused, Josh. Make me understand. When did you become a thug?
I don't know. I just was a little ang—

Are you going to get "angry" every time JB has a girlfriend?
It wasn't just that.

Then what was it? I'm waiting.
I don't know.

Okay, well, since you don't know, here's what I know—
I just got a little upset.

Not good enough. Your behavior was unacceptable.
I said I'm sorry.

Indeed you did. But you need to tell your brother, not me.
I will.

There are always consequences, Josh.
Here it comes: Dishes for a week, no phone, or, worse,
no Sundays at the Rec.

Josh, you and JB are growing up.
I know.

140

You're twins, not the same person.
But that doesn't mean he has to stop loving me.

Your brother will always love you, Josh.
I guess.

Boys with no discipline end up in prison.
Yeah, I heard you the first time.

Don't you get smart with me and end up in more trouble.
Why are you always trying to scare me?

We're done. Your dad is waiting for you.

Okay, but what are the consequences?

You're suspended.

From school?

From the team.

. . .

chur·lish

[CHUHR-LISH] *adjective*

Having a bad temper, and
being difficult to work with.

As in: I wanted a pair
of Stephon Marbury's sneakers
(Starburys),
but Dad called him
a selfish millionaire
with a bad attitude,
and why would I want
to be associated
with such a *churlish*
choke artist.

As in: I don't understand
how I went
from annoyed
to grumpy
to downright
churlish.

As in: How do you apologize
to your twin brother
for being *churlish* —
for almost
breaking
his nose?

This week, I

get my report card.
Make the honor roll.

Watch the team win
game nine.

Volunteer
at the library.

Eat lunch alone
five times.

Avoid
Miss Sweet Tea.

Walk home
by myself.

Clean the garage
during practice.

Try to atone
day and night.

Sit beside JB at dinner.
He moves.

Tell him a joke.
He doesn't even smile.

Do his chores.
He pays no attention.

Say I'm sorry
but he won't listen.

Basketball Rule #7

Rebounding
is the art
of anticipating,
of always being prepared
to grab it.
But you can't
drop the ball.

The Nosebleed Section

Our seats are in the clouds,
and every time Dad thinks
the ref makes a bad call,
he rains.
All Mom does is pop up
like an umbrella,
then Dad sits
back down.

JB's got nineteen points,
six rebounds,
and three assists.
He's on fire,
blazing from
baseline to baseline.
Dad screams,
Somebody needs to call
the fire department,
'cause JB is burning up
this place.

The other team calls a time-out.
Dad, JB still won't speak to me, I say.
Right now JB can't
see you, son, Dad says.

You just have to let the smoke
clear, and then he'll be okay.
For now, why don't you
write him a letter?
Good idea, I think.
But what should I say? I ask him.
By then,
Dad is on his feet
with the rest of the gym
as JB steals the ball
and takes off
like a wildfire.

Fast Break

He's a
Backcourt Baller
On the b r e a k,
a RUNNING GUNNING
SHOOTING ST AR
FLYING *F A S T.*
JB's FIXING for the GLASS —
BOUNCE BOUNCE   ball beside him
NOW he's GETTING
FLYER and FLYER,
CLIMBing   **sky.**
He nods his head
and pumps a *FAKE,*
Explodes the lane.
CRISS ball CROSS ball *CRISS*
and takes the break
K
   A
      B
        O
          O
            M

Above the rim,
A THUNDEROUS almost DUNK.
That elbow just sent JB
K
    E
       R
          P
             L
                U
                   N
                      K

to the floor.

F O U L.

Storm

Like a strong wind, Dad
rises from the clouds, strikes

down the stairs, swift and
sharp and mad as

lightning. *Flagrant foul, ref!*
he yells to everyone in the

gym. Now he's hail and blizzard.
His face, cold and hard as ice.

His hands pulsing through
the air. His mouth, loud as thunder.

He tackled JB—
this ain't football,

Dad roars in the face
of the ref, while JB

and his attacker do
the eye dance. I want to

join in, offer my squall,
but Mom shoots me a look

that says, *Stay out of the rain,
son.* So, I just watch

as she and Coach chase
Dad's tornado. I watch

as she wraps her arms
around Dad's waist. I watch

as she slowly brings him back
to wind and cloud. I watch

Mom take a tissue from
her purse to wipe her tears,

and the sudden onset of
blood from Dad's nose.

The next morning

at breakfast
Mom tells Dad,
Call Dr. Youngblood today   *or else.*

The name's ironic, I think.

*I'm sorry for losing
my cool,*
Dad tells us.

JB asks Mom
can he go to the mall
after practice today?

There's a new video game
we can check out,
I say to JB.

He hasn't spoken to me in five days.

*Your brother has apologized
profusely for his mistake,*
Mom says to JB.

*Tell him that I saw the look
in his eyes, and it wasn't a mistake,*
JB replies.

pro·fuse·ly

[PRUH-FYOOS-LEE] *adverb*

Pouring forth
in great quantity.

As in: JB gets all nervous and
sweats *profusely*
every time
Miss Sweet Tea walks
into a room.

154   As in: The team has thanked
JB *profusely*
for leading us
into
the playoffs.

As in: Mom said
Dad's blood pressure
was so high
during the game that when
he went into a rage
it caused
his nose
to start bleeding
profusely.

Article #1 in the *Daily News* (December 14)

The Reggie Lewis Wildcats
capped off their remarkable season
with a fiery win against
Olive Branch Junior High.
Playing without suspended phenom
Josh Bell didn't seem to faze
Coach Hawkins' undefeated 'Cats.
After a brief melee caused by a hard foul,
Josh's twin, Jordan, led the team,
like GW crossing the Delaware,
to victory, and to their
second straight playoff appearance.
With a first-round bye,
they begin their quest
for the county trophy
next week
against the Independence Red Rockets,
the defending champions,
while playing without
Josh "Filthy McNasty" Bell
the *Daily News*'s
Most Valuable Player.

Mostly everyone

in class applauds,
congratulating me
on being selected
as the Junior High MVP
by the *Daily News*.

Everyone except
Miss Sweet Tea:

YOU'RE MEAN, JOSH!
And I don't know why
they gave you that award
after what you did to Jordan.
JERK!

JB looks at me.
I wait for him to say *something, anything*
in defense of his only brother.
But his eyes, empty as fired cannons,
shoot way past me.

Sometimes it's the things that aren't said
that kill you.

Final Jeopardy

The only sounds,
teeth munching melon and strawberry
from Mom's fruit cocktail dessert

and Alex Trebek's annoying voice:
This fourteen-time NBA all-star
also played minor-league baseball

for the Birmingham Barons.
Even Mom knows the answer.
Hey, Dad, the playoffs start in two days

and the team needs me, I say.
Plus my grades were good.
JB rolls his eyes and says to Alex

what we all know: Who is "Michael Jeffrey Jordan"?
Josh, this isn't about your grades, Mom says.
How you behave going forward is what matters to us.

I loooove Christmas.
Can't wait for your mother's
maple turkey, Dad says, trying

to break the tension. Nobody responds,
so he continues:
Y'all know what the mama turkey

said to her naughty son?
If your papa could see you now,
he'd turn over in his gravy!

None of us laughs.
Then all of us laugh.
Chuck, you are a silly man, Mom says.

Jordan, we want to meet your new friend, she adds.

Yeah, invite her to dinner, Dad agrees.
Filthy and I
want to get to know the girl who stole JB.

Stop that, Chuck! Mom says, hitting Dad on the arm.
What is "I'll think about it"? JB replies,
kissing Mom, dapping Dad, and not once

looking
at
me.

Dear Jordan

without u

    i am empty,

the goal

    with no net.

seems

    my life was

broken,

    shattered,

like puzzle pieces

    on the court.

i can no longer fit.

    can you

help me heal,

    run with me,

slash with me

    like we used to?

like two stars

    stealing sun,

like two brothers

    burning up.

together.

PS. I'm sorry.

I don't know

if he read
my letter,
but this morning
on the bus
to school
when I said,
Vondie, your head
is so big,
you don't have a forehead,
you have a five-head,
I could feel
JB laughing
a little.

No Pizza and Fries

The spinach
and tofu
salad
Mom packed
for my lunch
today is cruel,
but not as cruel
as the evil look
Miss Sweet Tea
shoots me
from across
the cafeteria.

Even Vondie

has a girlfriend now.
She wants to be a doctor one day.

She's a candy striper
and a cheerleader
and a talker

with skinny legs
and a butt
as big
as Vermont,

which according to her
has the best tomatoes,

which she claims
come in all colors,
even purple,

which she tells me
is her favorite color,
which I already know
because of her hair.

This is still better
than having
no girlfriend at all.

Which is what I have
now.

Uh-oh

While I'm on the phone
with Vondie
talking about
my chances of playing
in another game
this season,
I hear panting
coming from Mom
and Dad's room,
but we don't own
a dog.

I run into Dad's room

to see what all the noise is
and find him kneeling
on the floor, rubbing a towel

in the rug. It reeks of vomit.
You threw up, Dad? I ask.
Must have been something I ate.

He sits up on the bed, holds
his chest like he's pledging
allegiance. Only there's no flag.

Y'all ready to eat? he mutters.
You okay, Dad? I ask.
He nods and shows me

a letter he's reading.
Dad, was that you coughing?
I've got great news, Filthy.

What is it? I ask.
*I got a coaching offer at a nearby
college starting next month.*

A job? What about the house?
What about Mom? What about me
and JB? Who's gonna shoot

free throws with us every night? I ask.
Filthy, you and JB are getting older,
more mature—you'll manage, he says.

And, what's with the switch? First
you want me to get a job, now
you don't? What's up, Filthy?

Dad, Mom thinks you should
take it easy, for your health, right?
I mean, didn't you make a million dollars

playing basketball? You don't
really need to work.
Filthy, what I need is to get back

on the court. That's what your dad NEEDS!
I prefer to be called Josh, Dad.
Not Filthy.

Oh, really, Filthy? he laughs.
I'm serious, Dad—please don't call me
that name anymore.

You gonna take the job, Dad?
Son, I miss "swish."
I miss the smell of orange leather.

I miss eatin' up cats
who think they can run with Da Man.
The court is my kitchen.

Son, I miss being the top chef.
So, yeah, I'm gonna take it . . .
if your mother lets me.

Well, I will talk to her about
this job thing, since it means
so much to you. But, you know

she's really worried about you, Dad.
Filth — I mean Josh, okay, you talk
to her, he laughs.

And maybe, in return, Dad, you can talk
to her about letting me back on the team
for the playoffs.

I feel like
I'm letting my teammates down.
You let your family down too, Josh, he replies,

still holding his chest.
So what should I do, Dad? I ask.
Well, right now you should

go set the dinner table, Mom says,
standing at the door
watching Dad with eyes

full of panic.

Behind Closed Doors

We decided no more basketball, Chuck, Mom yells.
Baby, it's not ball, it's coaching, Dad tells her.

It's still stress. You don't need to be on the court.
The doctor said it's fine, baby.

What doctor? When did you go to the doctor?
I go a couple times a week. Dr. WebMD.

Are you serious! This is not some joke, Charles.
. . .

Going online is not going to save your life.
Truth is, I've had enough of this talk about me being sick.

So have I. I'm scheduling an appointment for you.
Fine!

*I shouldn't be so worried about your heart—it's your head
that's crazy.*
Crazy for you, lil' mama.

Stop that. I said stop. It's time for dinner, Chuck . . . oooh.
Who's Da Man?

And then there is silence, so I go set the dinner table,
because when they stop talking,

I know what that means.
Uggghh!

The girl who stole my brother

is her new name.
She's no longer sweet.
Bitter is her taste.
Even worse,
she asks for seconds
of vegetable lasagna,
which makes Mom smile
'cause JB and I can't get with
this whole better-eating thing
and we never ask for seconds

until tonight, when JB,
still grinning and cheesing
for some invisible camera
that Miss Bitter (Sweet) Tea holds,
asks for more salad,
which makes Dad laugh
and prompts Mom
to ask,
How did you two meet?

Surprisingly, JB is a motor mouth,
giving us all the details about
that first time in the cafeteria:

She came into the lunchroom.
It was her first day at our school,
and we just started talking about
all kinds of stuff, and she said she played
basketball at her last school, and then
Vondie was like, "JB, she's hot," and
I was like, "Yeah, she is kinda
pulchritudinous."
And for the first time
in fifteen days, JB looks
at me for a split second,
and I almost see
the hint of a
smile.

Things I Learn at Dinner

She went to Nike Hoops Camp for Girls.

Her favorite player is Skylar Diggins.

She can name each of the 2010 NBA Champion Lakers.

Her dad went to college with Shaquille O'Neal.

She knows how to do a crossover.

Her AAU team won a championship.

She's got game.

Her parents are divorced.

She's going to visit her mom next week for Christmas break.

She lives with her dad.

She shoots hoop at the Rec to relax.

Her mom doesn't want her playing basketball.

Her dad's coming to our game tomorrow to see JB play.

She's sorry I won't be playing.

Her smile is as sweet as Mom's carrot cake.

She smells like sugarplum.

She has a sister in college.

HER SISTER GOES TO DUKE.

Dishes

When the last plate is scrubbed,
the leftovers put up,
and the floor swept clean,
Mom comes into the kitchen.
When is Dad's doctor appointment? I ask.
Josh, you know I don't like
you eavesdropping.
I get it from you, Mom, I say.
And she laughs, 'cause she knows
I'm not saying nothing but the truth.
It's next week.
School's out next week.
Maybe I can go
with you
to the doctor?
Maybe, she says.

I put the broom down,
wrap my arms around her,
and tell her thank you.
For loving us, and Dad, and
letting us play basketball,
and being the best mother
in the world.

Keep this up, she says, *and*
you'll be back on the court
in no time.

Does that mean
I can play in tomorrow's
playoff game? I ask.
Don't press your luck, son.
It's going to take more than a hug.
Now help me dry these dishes.

Coach's Talk Before the Game

Tonight
I decide to sit
on the bench
with the team
during the game
instead of the bleachers
with Dad
and Mom, who's sitting
next to him
just in case
he decides to
act churlish
again.

Coach says:
We've won
ten games
in a row.
The difference between
a winning streak
and a losing streak
is one game.

Now, Josh is not with us
again, so somebody's
gonna have to step up
in the low post.

I sit back down
on the bench
and watch JB lead our Wildcats
to the court.
When the game finally starts,
I glance up at Dad and Mom,
but they're not there.
When I look back
at the court,
JB is staring at me
like we've both just seen
another ghost.

Josh's Play-by-Play

The team's in trouble.
If they don't find an answer soon
our championship dreams are over.
Down by three, they're playing
like kittens, not Wildcats.
With less than a minute to go
Vondie brings the ball up the court.
Will he go inside for a quick two
or get the ball to JB
for the three-ball?
He passes the ball to number twenty-nine
on the right wing
and tries to dribble out,
but the defense is suffocating.
They're on him like
black on midnight.
He shoots it over to JB,
who looks up at the clock.
He's gonna let it get as close
as possible.
They've gotta miss me right now.
Vondie comes over, sets a high pick.
JB's open, he's gonna take the three.
It's up.
That's a good-looking ball there.

But not good enough.
It clangs off the rim.
The buzzer
rings
and the Wildcats
lose
the first half.

Text Messages from Mom, Part One

7:04
Dad wasn't feeling
well, so we went outside
for some air. Back soon.

7:17
I think we're
heading home. At halftime,
let your brother know.

7:45
Home now. Dad wants
to know the score. How is Jordan
doing? You okay?

7:47
Y'all hang in there. The
second half will be better.
Hi to Alexis. Get

7:47
a ride with Coach
or Vondie. Yes, Dad's okay.
I think. See you soon.

7:48

I shouldn't have said
"I think." He's fine, just tired.
He says don't come home

7:48

if you lose. LOL.

The Second Half

Vondie strips the ball
at center court,
shoots a short pass
to JB, who
skips

       downtown
zips

       around,
then double dips
it in the bowl.

SWOOSH.

Man, that was cold.
We're up by two.
These cats are BALLING.
JB is on fire,
taking the score
higher and higher,
and the team
and Coach
and Alexis
and me . . .
we're his choir.
WILDCATS! WILDCATS!
My brother is
Superman tonight,

Sliding
and Gliding
into rare air,
lighting up the sky
and the scoreboard.
Saving the world
and our chance
at a championship.

Tomorrow Is the Last Day of School Before Christmas Vacation

Tonight, I'm studying.
Usually I help JB
prepare for his tests,
but since the incident
he's been studying alone,
which has me a little scared
because tomorrow is also the big
vocabulary standards test.
(But don't say that word
around Mom. She thinks
that "standards" are a lousy idea).

So, after the game
I go home and pull out
my study sheet with all
the words
we've been studying
and my clues
to remember them.
Like *heirloom*.
As in: Dad treats his championship ring
like some kind of family *heirloom*
that we can't wear
until one of us becomes *Da Man*.

I put eight pages of words
on JB's pillow
while he's brushing
his teeth,
then turn off my light
and go to sleep.
When he climbs into bed,
I hear the sound of ruffling paper.
Then his night-light comes on
and I don't hear anything else
except
Thanks.

Coach comes over

to my table
during lunch,
sits down
with a bag
from McDonald's,
hands me a fry
and Vondie a fry,
bites into his
McRib sandwich,
and says:
Look, Josh,
you and your brother need
to squash this beef.
If my two stars
aren't aligned,
there's no way
the universe is kind to us.

Huh? Vondie says.

My brother and I
got into a bad fight
when we were in high school,

and we've been estranged
ever since.
You want that?

I shake my head.

Then fix it, Filthy.
Fix it fast.
We don't need any distractions
on this journey.
And while you're working
on that, give your mom
something special this holiday.

She says you've served
your sentence well
and that she'll consider
letting you back
on the team
if we make it
to the championship game.
Merry Christmas, Josh.

es·tranged

[IH-STREYNJD] *adjective*

The interruption of a bond,
when one person becomes
a stranger
to someone
who was close:
a relative, friend,
or loved one.

As in: Alexis's mom and dad
are *estranged.*

As in: When I threw the ball
at JB,
I think I was *estranged*
from myself,
if that's possible.

As in: Even though JB and I
are *estranged,*
Dad's making us play
together
in a three-on-three tournament
on the Rec playground
tomorrow.

School's Out

Mom has to work late,
so Dad picks us up.
Even though JB's
still not talking to me
Dad's cracking jokes
and we're both laughing
like it's the good ol' times.
What are we getting for Christmas, Dad? JB asks.
What we always get. Books, I reply,
and we both laugh

just like the good ol' times.
Boys, your talent will help you win games, Dad says,
but your intelligence, that will help you win at life.
Who said that? I ask.
I said it, didn't you hear me?
Michael Jordan said it, JB says,
still looking at Dad.
Look, boys, you've both done good
in school this year, and
your mom and I appreciate that.
So you choose a gift, and I'll get it.
You mean no books? I ask. Yes!
Nope. You're still getting the books, player.
Santa's just letting you pick something extra.
At the stoplight,

JB and I look out
the window
at the exact moment
we pass by the mall
and I know exactly
what JB wants.
Dad, can we stop
at that sneaker store
in the mall?
Yeah, Dad, can we? JB echoes.
And the word *we*
never sounded
sweeter.

The Phone Rings

Mom's decorating the tree,
Dad's outside shooting free throws,
warming up for the tournament.
Hello, I answer.
Hi, Josh, she replies.
*May I please speak
with Precious?*
He's, uh, busy right now,
I tell her.
Well, just tell him
I will see him at the Rec,
she says, and now
I understand
why JB's
taking his second shower
this morning
when he barely takes ONE
most school mornings.

Basketball Rule #8

Sometimes
you have to
lean back
a little
and
fade away
to get
the best
shot.

191

When we get to the court

I challenge Dad
to a quick game
of one-on-one
before the tournament
so we can both warm up.
He laughs and says, *Check,*
then gives me the ball,
but it hits me in the chest
because I'm busy looking over
at the swings where Jordan and

Miss Sweet Tea are talking
and holding hands.
Pay attention, Filthy—I mean Josh.
I'm about to CLEAN you up, boy, Dad says.
I pump fake him then sugar shake him
for an easy two. I hear applause.
Kids are coming over to watch.
On the next play I switch it up
and launch a three from downtown.
It rolls round and round and IN.
The benches are filling up.
Even Jordan and Alexis are now watching.
Five-oh is the score,
third play of the game.
I try my crossover, but

Dad steals the ball
like a thief in the night,
camps out at the top for a minute.
What you doing, old man? I say.
Don't worry 'bout me, son.
I'm contemplatin',
preparing to shut down
all your playa hatin', Dad says.
Son, I ever tell you
about this cat named
Willie I played with in Italy?
And before I can answer
he unleashes a
killer crossover,
leaving me wishing for a cushion.
The kids are off the benches.
On their feet hollerin',
Ohhhhhhhhhh, Whoop Whoop!
Meet the Press, Josh Bell, Dad laughs,
on his way to the hoop.
But then —

At Noon, in the Gym, with Dad

People watching
Players boasting
Me scoring
Dad snoring
Crowd growing
We balling
Me pumping
Dad jumping
Me faking
Nasty shot
Nasty moves
Five–zero
My lead
Next play
Dribble bounce
Dribble steal
Dad laughs
Palms ball
You okay?
Dad winks
Watch this
He dips
Sweat drips
Left y'all
Right y'all

I fall
Crowd wild
Dad drives
Steps strides
Runs fast
Hoop bound
Stutter steps
Lets loose
Screams loud
Stands still
Breath short
More sweat
Grabs chest
Eyes roll
Ball drops
Dad drops
I scream
"Help, please"
Sweet Tea
Dials cell
Jordan runs
Brings water
Splashes face
Dad nothing
Out cold
I remember
Gym class
Tilt pinch

Blow pump
Blow pump
Still nothing
Blow pump
Sirens blast
Pulse gone
Eyes shut.

FOURTH QUARTER

The doctor pats Jordan and me
on the back and says

Your dad should be fine. If you're lucky,
you boys will be fishing with him in no time.

We don't fish, I tell him.
Mom shoots me a mean look.

Mrs. Bell, the myocardial infarction has caused some
complications. Your husband's stable, but he is in a coma.

In between sobs, JB barely gets his question out:
Will my dad be home for Christmas?

He looks at us and says: *Try talking to him,*
maybe he can hear you, which could help him come back.

Well, MAYBE we're not in a talking mood, I say.
Joshua Bell, be respectful! Mom tells me.

I shouldn't even be here.
I should be putting on my uniform, stretching,

getting ready to play in the county semifinals.
But instead, I'm sitting in a smelly room

in St. Luke's Hospital,
listening to Mom sing "Kumbaya,"

watching Jordan hold Dad's hand,
wondering why I have

to push water uphill
with a rake

to talk to someone
who isn't even listening.

To miss the biggest game
of my life.

my·o·car·di·al in·farc·tion

[MY-OH-CAR-DEE-YUHL IN-FARK-SHUN] *noun*

Occurs when blood flow
to an area of the heart
is blocked
for a long enough time
that part of the heart muscle
is damaged
or dies.

As in: JB says that he hates
basketball because it was
the one thing that
Dad loved the most
besides us
and it was the one thing
that caused his
myocardial infarction.

As in: The doctor sees me Googling
the symptoms—coughing, sweating,
vomiting, nosebleeds—and he says,
You know we can't be sure what causes
a myocardial infarction. I say, What about
doughnuts and fried chicken and genetics?

The doctor looks at my mom,
then leaves.

As in: Dad's in a coma
because of a *myocardial infarction,*
which is the same thing
my grandfather died of.
So what does that mean for me
and JB?

Okay, Dad

The doctor says
I should talk to you,
that maybe you can hear
and maybe you can't.
Mom and JB
have been talking
your ear off
all morning.
So, if you're listening,
I'd like to know,
when did you decide to jump
ship? I thought you were
Da Man.
And one more thing:
If we make it
to the finals,
I will not miss
the big game
for a small

maybe.

Mom, since you asked, I'll tell you why I'm so angry

Because Dad tried to dunk.

Because I want to win a championship.

Because I can't win a championship if I'm sitting in this smelly hospital.

Because Dad told you he'd be here forever.

Because I thought forever was like Mars — far away.

Because it turns out forever is like the mall — right around the corner.

Because Jordan doesn't talk basketball anymore.

Because Jordan cut my hair and didn't care.

Because he's always drinking Sweet Tea.

Because sometimes I get thirsty.

Because I don't have anybody to talk to now.

Because I feel empty with no hair.

Because CPR DOESN'T WORK!

Because my crossover should be better.

Because if it was better, then Dad wouldn't have had the ball.

Because if Dad hadn't had the ball, then he wouldn't have tried to dunk.

Because if Dad hadn't tried to dunk, then we wouldn't be here.

Because I don't want to be *here*.

Because the only thing that matters is *swish*.

Because our backboard is splintered.

Text Messages from Vondie

8:05
Filthy, the game went
double overtime
before the last possession.

8:05
Coach called a time-out
and had us all do a special chant
on the sideline.

8:06
It was kinda creepy. The
other team was LOL.
I guess it worked, 'cause

8:06
we won, 40–39.
We dedicated the game ball
to your pop.

8:07
Is he better? You and JB
coming to practice?
Filthy, you there?

On Christmas Eve

Dad finally wakes up. He
smiles at

Mom, high-fives Jordan,
then looks right at me

and says,
Filthy, I didn't jump ship.

Santa Claus Stops By

We're celebrating
Christmas
in Dad's hospital room.
Flowers and gifts and cheer
surround him. Relatives from
five states. Aunts with collards and yams,
cousins with hoots and hollers,
and runny noses. Mom's singing,
Dad's playing spades with his brothers.
I know the nurses can't wait for visiting hours
to end. I can't either. Uncle Bob's turkey
tastes like cardboard
and his lemon pound cake looks like Jell-O, but
Hospital Santa has everyone singing and
all this joy is spoiling my mood. I can't
remember the last time I smiled. Happy is
a huge river right now and I've forgotten
how to swim. After two hours, Mom
tells everyone it's time for Dad to
get some rest. I hug fourteen people, which is
like drowning. When they leave, Dad
calls Jordan and me over to the bed.

Do y'all remember
when you were seven and JB
wanted to swing but all the swings were
filled, and Filthy pushed the little redhead
kid out of the swing so JB could take it?
Well, it wasn't the right behavior, but
the intention was righteous.
You were there for each other.
I want you both
to always be there
for each other.

Jordan starts crying.
Mom holds him,
and takes him outside
for a walk.
Me and Dad stare
at each other
for ten minutes
without saying a word.
I tell him,
I don't have anything to say.

Filthy, silence doesn't mean
we have run out of things to say,
only that we are trying
not to say them.
So, let's do this.

I'll ask you a question,
then you ask me a question,
and we'll just keep asking until
we can both get some answers.
Okay?

Sure, I say,
but you go first.

Questions

Have you been practicing your free throws?
Why didn't you go to the doctor when Mom asked you?

When is the game?
Why didn't you ever take us fishing?

Does your brother still have a girlfriend?
Are you going to die?

Do you really want to know?
Why couldn't I save you?

Don't you see that you did?
Do you remember I kept pumping and breathing?

Aren't I alive?
. . . ?

*Did y'all arrest Uncle Bob's turkey? It was just criminal
    what he did to that bird, wasn't it?*
You think this is funny?

How's your brother?
Is our family falling apart?

You still think I should write a book?
What does that have to do with anything?

What if I call it "Basketball Rules"?
Are you going to die?

Do you know I love you, son?
Don't you know the big game's tomorrow?

Is it true Mom is letting you play?
You think I shouldn't play?

What do you think, Filthy?
What about Jordan?

Does he want to play?
Don't you know he won't as long as you're in here?

Don't you know I know that?
So, why don't you come home?

Can't you see I can't?
Why not?

Don't you know it's complicated, Filthy?
Why can't you call me by my real name?

Josh, do you know what a heart attack is?
Don't you remember I was there?

*Don't you see I need to be here so they can fix the
    damage that's been done to my heart?*
Who's gonna fix the damage that's been done to mine?

Tanka for Language Arts Class

This Christmas was not
Merry, and I have not found
joy in the new year
with Dad in the hospital
for nineteen days and counting.

I don't think I'll ever get used to

walking home from school   alone
playing Madden   alone

listening to Lil Wayne   alone
going to the library   alone

shooting free throws   alone
watching ESPN   alone

eating doughnuts   alone
saying my prayers   alone

Now that Jordan's in love
and Dad's living in a hospital

Basketball Rule #9

When the game is on
the line,
don't fear.
Grab the ball.
Take it
to the hoop.

As we're about to leave for the final game

the phone rings.
Mom shrieks.
I think the worst.
I ask JB if he heard *that*.
He's on his bunk
listening to his iPod.
Mom rushes past our room,
out of breath.
JB jumps down
from his bunk.
What's wrong, Mom? I ask.

She says:
Dad. Had. Another. Attack.
Now. Don't. Worry.
I'm. Going. Hospital.
See. You. Two. At. Game.

Vroooooommmmmmm.
Her car starts.
JB, what should we do? I ask.

He's no longer listening to music,
but his tears are loud enough
to dance to.

He laces his sneakers,
runs out of our room.
The garage door opens.
I hear FLOP FLOP FLOP
from the straws
on the spokes
of his bicycle wheels
as he follows Mom
to the hospital.

I hear the clock: TICK TOCK TICK TOCK.
I hear Dad: *You should play in the game, son.*
A horn blows.

I hear SLAM SLAM SLAM
as I shut the door
of Vondie's dad's car.
I hear SCREECH SCREECH SCREECH
as we pull away
from the curb
on our way
to the county championship game.

During warm-ups

I miss four lay-ups in
a row, and Coach Hawkins says,
Josh, you sure you're able

to play? It's more than okay if you
need to go to the hospital with your fam—
Coach, my dad is going to be fine,

I say. Plus he wants me to play.
Son, you telling me you're okay?
Can a deaf person write

music? I ask Coach.
He raises his eyebrows,
shakes his head, and

tells me to go sit
on the bench. I excuse myself
to the locker room

to check my cell phone,
and there are texts
from Mom.

Text Messages from Mom, Part Two

5:47
Dad's having complications.
But he's gonna
be fine and says
he loves you.
Good luck tonight. Dad's

5:47
gonna be fine. Jordan says
he still doesn't feel like
playing, but I made him

5:48
go to the game to show
support. Look for him and
don't get lazy on your

5:48
crossover.

For Dad

My free throw flirts with the rim and
loops, twirls, for a million years,

then drops, and for once, we're up, 49–48,
five dancers on stage, leaping, jumping

so high, so fly,
eleven seconds from sky

A hard drive, a fast break, their best player
slices the thick air toward the goal.

His pull-up jumper
floats through the net,

then everything goes slow motion:
the ball, the player . . .

Coach calls time-out
with only five seconds to go.

I wish the ref could stop
the clock of my life.

Just one more game.
I think my father is dying,

and now I am out of bounds
when I see a familiar face

behind our bench. My brother,
Jordan Bell, head buried

in Sweet Tea, his eyes
welling with horror.

Before I know it, the whistle blows,
the ball in my hand,

the clock running down,
my tears running faster.

The Last Shot

5 . . . A bolt of lightning on my kicks . . .

The court is   SIZZLING

My sweat is   DRIZZLING

Stop all that *quivering*

Cuz tonight I'm *delivering*

I'm driving down

                    the lane

SLIDING

4 . . . Dribbling to the middle, gliding like a black eagle.

The crowd is RUMBLING RUSTLING

ROARING

Take it to the hoop.

TAKE   IT   TO   THE   HOOP

3 . . . *2* . . . Watch out, 'cuz I'm about to get D I R T Y

with it

about to pour FILTHY'S sauce all over you.

Ohhhhh, did you see McNASTY cross over you?

Now I'm taking you

Ankle BREAKING you

You're on your knees.

Screamin' PLEASE, BABY, PLEASE

One . . . It's a bird, It's a plane. No, it's up up
uppppppppppp.
My shot is F L O W I N G, Flying, fLuTtErInG
OHHHHHHHH, the chains are JINGALING
ringaling and SWINGALING
Swish.

Game/over.

OVERTIME

Article #2 in the *Daily News* (January 14)

Professional basketball player
Charlie (Chuck) "Da Man" Bell
collapsed in a game
of one-on-one
with his son Josh.
After a complication,
Bell died at St. Luke's Hospital
from a massive heart attack.

According to reports,
Bell suffered
from hypertension
and had three fainting spells
in the four months
before his collapse.
Autopsy results found
Bell had a large,
extensively scarred heart.
Reports have surfaced
that Bell refused to see a doctor.
One of his former teammates
stated, "He wasn't a big fan of doctors
and hospitals, that's for sure."

Earlier in his life,
Bell chose to end his promising basketball career
rather than have surgery on his knee.

Known for his dazzling crossover,
Chuck Bell was the captain
of the Italian team
that won back-to-back Euroleague championships
in the late nineties.
He is survived by his wife,
Dr. Crystal Stanley-Bell, and
his twin sons,
Joshua and Jordan, who
recently won their first
county championship.
Bell was thirty-nine.

Where Do We Go from Here?

There are no coaches
at funerals. No practice
to get ready. No warm-up.
There is no last-second shot, and
we all wear its cruel
midnight uniform, starless
and unfriendly.

I am unprepared
for death.
This is a game
I cannot play.
It has no rules,
no referees.
You cannot win.

I listen
to my father's teammates
tell funny stories
about love
and basketball.
I hear the choir's comfort songs.
They almost drown out Mom's sobs.

She will not look in the coffin.
That is not my husband, she says.
Dad is gone,
like the end of a good song.
What remains is bone
and muscle and cold skin.
I grab Mom's right hand.
JB grabs her left.
The preacher says,
A great father, son, and
husband has crossed
over. Amen.
Outside, a long charcoal limo
pulls up to the curb
to take us
back.

If only.

star·less

[STAHR-LES] *adjective*

With no stars.

As in: If me and JB
try out for JV
next year,
the Reggie Lewis Junior High School Wildcats
will be *starless.*

As in: Last night
I felt like I was fading away
as I watched the *starless*
Portland Trailblazers
get stomped by Dad's favorite team,
the Lakers.

As in: My father
was the light
of my world,
and now that he's gone,
each night
is *starless.*

Basketball Rule #10

A loss is inevitable,
like snow in winter.
True champions
learn
to dance
through
the storm.

There are so many friends

neighbors, Dad's teammates,
and family members
packed into our living room
that I have to go outside
just to breathe. The air
is filled with laughter,
John Coltrane,
Jay-Z, and the smell
of salmon, plus scents of
every pie and cake
imaginable.

Even Mom is smiling.
Josh, don't you hear the phone
ringing? she says.
I don't—the sound of
"A Love Supreme"
and loud laughter
drowning it out.
Can you get it, please? she asks me.

I answer it, a salmon sandwich
crammed in my mouth.
Hello, Bell residence, I mutter.
Hi, this is Alexis.

Oh . . . Hey.
I'm sorry I couldn't be at the funeral.
This is Josh, not JB.
I know it's you, Filthy. JB is loud.
Your phone voice always sounds like
it's the break of dawn,
like you're just waking up,
she says playfully.
I laugh for the first time in days.
I just wanted to call and say how sorry
I am for your loss. If there is anything my dad or I can do,
please let us know.
Look, Alexis, I'm sorry about—

It's all good, Filthy. I gotta go, but
my sister has five tickets
to see Duke play North Carolina.
Me, her, JB, and my dad
are going.
You wanna—
ABSOLUTELY, I say, and THANKS,
right before Coach Hawkins
comes my way
with outstretched arms and
a bear-size hug, sending the phone
crashing to the floor.

On my way out the door,
to get some fresh air,
Mom gives me
a kiss and a piece of
sweet potato pie with
two scoops of vanilla soy
ice cream.
Where's your brother? she asks.

I haven't seen JB
since the funeral, but
if I had to guess, I'd say
he's going to see Alexis.
Because, if I had a girlfriend, I'd be
off with her right about now.
But I don't,
so the next best thing
will have to do.

Free Throws

It only takes me
Four mouthfuls
to finish the dessert.
I have to jump to get the ball.
It is wedged between
rim and backboard,
evidence of JB trying
and failing
to dunk.
I tap it out

and dribble
to the free-throw line.

Dad once made
fifty free throws
IN A ROW.
The most I ever made
was nineteen.
I grip the ball,
plant my feet on the line,
and shoot the first one.
It goes in.
I look around
to see if anyone is watching.
Nope. Not anymore.

The next twelve shots are good.
I name them each a year
in my life.
A year with my father.
By twenty-seven, I am making them
with my eyes closed.
The orange orb has wings
like there's an angel
taking it to the hoop.

On the forty-ninth shot,
I am only slightly aware
that I am moments from fifty.
The only thing that really matters
is that out here
in the driveway
shooting free throws
I feel closer to Dad.

You feel better? he asks.

Dad? I say.
I open my eyes,
and there is my brother.
I thought you were—

Yeah, I know, he says.

I'm good. You? I ask.
He nods.
Good game last week, he says.
That crossover
was wicked.

Did you see the trophy? I ask.
He nods again.
Still protecting his words
from me.
Did you talk to Dad before—
He told us to stay out of his closet.
Then he told me to give you this.
You earned it, Filthy, he says,
sliding the ring on my finger.
My heart leaps
into my throat.

Dad's championship ring.
Between the bouncing
and sobbing, I whisper, Why?

I guess you Da Man now, Filthy, JB says.

And for the first time in my life
I don't want to be.

I bet
the dishes
you miss number fifty, he says,
walking away.

Where's he going?

Hey, I shout.
We Da Man.
And when he turns around
I toss him the ball.

He dribbles
back to the top of the key,
fixes his eyes
on the goal.
I watch
the ball
leave his hands
like a bird
up high,
skating
the sky,

crossing over
us.

PRAISE FOR *THE CROSSOVER*

"*The Crossover* is a masterful mix of rhythm and heart that tells the story of two brothers navigating the deep waters of love, loyalty, and championship play. Alexander's verse is fluid and electric, poignant and wise."

—JOYCE SIDMAN, NEWBERY HONOR–WINNING AUTHOR OF *DARK EMPEROR AND OTHER POEMS OF THE NIGHT*

"The characters of Kwame Alexander's verse novel entered my heart, as it showed the many ways in which the basketball, the truth, love, and life cross over and between us."

—MARILYN NELSON, NEWBERY HONOR–WINNING AUTHOR OF *CARVER: A LIFE IN POEMS*

"Kwame Alexander's sizzling, heartfelt story in verse, *The Crossover*, gives readers that rich sense of *SWISH!* we feel when a basketball drops perfectly through a net. Quick timing, snazzy cadence, a wealth of energy, and deep affection for sports, family, and life in general—it's all here, in these gripping scenes."

—NAOMI SHIHAB NYE, NATIONAL BOOK AWARD FINALIST

"A basketball novel, yes, but also a story of family, dedication, loyalty, loss, and redemption, wrapped up in a slam dunk of powerful language."

—KATHRYN ERSKINE, AUTHOR OF *MOCKINGBIRD*, A NATIONAL BOOK AWARD WINNER

"You don't have to be a basketball fan to feel the exhilaration of a game well played in Kwame Alexander's novel. You don't have to be a poetry fan either to appreciate the verve and variety of his verse, but chances are, after reading this book, you'll become one."

—MARILYN SINGER, AUTHOR OF *MIRROR MIRROR* AND *FOLLOW FOLLOW*

"*The Crossover* crosses over as a gift to all ages."

—ASHLEY BRYAN, TWO-TIME CORETTA SCOTT KING AWARD WINNER